This book belongs to

_____

LITTLE CHICK'S
EASTER TREASURE

Illustrated by

Walt Sturrock

Story by

Samantha Shaw

The Unicorn Publishing House
New Jersey

LITTLE CHICK'S EASTER TREASURE

Spring had come early this year. The flowers bloomed everywhere. Little Chick (and indeed she was a little chick, for this was her VERY first spring) had been running and skipping through the fields picking all the pretty flowers she could find. Having filled her basket full, Little Chick decided to head home.

LITTLE CHICK'S EASTER TREASURE

Along the way, Little Chick met two small bunnies picking berries. Little Chick was CURIOUS, for she thought bunnies only ate grass and juicy carrots.

"Why are you picking berries?" Little Chick asked.

"For the Easter Eggs, of course," Black Bunny said. "We have to color the eggs, you know, for the Egg Hunt tomorrow."

"The Egg Hunt?" Little Chick said with wonder. "What Egg Hunt?"

"You DON'T know!" both bunnies said, their eyes wide with surprise. "Well, you'll find out tomorrow." And before Little Chick could say another word, the two bunnies hopped away into the woods.

Then remembering that Grandpa Redcomb would be waiting, Little Chick hurried off towards home.

LITTLE CHICK'S EASTER TREASURE

Little Chick was in such a hurry that all the flowers she had picked FELL out of her basket along the way. But Little Chick didn't have time to stop, for Grandpa Redcomb would be telling one of his stories, and she wouldn't miss one of his tales for anything.

Grandpa Redcomb was a seafaring rooster and a teller of tall tales. Seeing Little Chick running up the path, he called out: "Hurry, honey, and jump up on my leg. I don't want to start without you."

Grandpa Redcomb didn't tell them about pirates or monsters, or even buried treasure—like he usually did. No. He told them about a Great Easter Egg Hunt and a beautiful Golden Egg. He said that when he was a small chick, no bigger than Little Chick, he went on the Egg Hunt. Now Grandpa Redcomb loved a good tale, and true or not, he told them that HE had found the Golden Egg and won a Blue Ribbon as first prize. All the young animals' eyes opened wide with excitement. But no one's eyes grew wider than Little Chick's, for she WANTED to find the Golden Egg just like Grandpa Redcomb—and the Great Easter Egg Hunt was TOMORROW!

LITTLE CHICK'S EASTER TREASURE

Night fell, and Little Chick undressed and climbed into bed. But she couldn't sleep. She could only think of the Great Egg Hunt the next day.

Mama Hen came in to kiss her goodnight and saw how excited her Little Chick was.

"Mama, do you think I WILL be the one to find the Golden Egg?" Little Chick asked.

"Why, of course you might, honey. But I know that a Little Chick who has had her sleep will have a better chance than a sleepy one. Now try to sleep, little one," Mama Hen said, and she sweetly chirped a lullaby till at last Little Chick fell asleep and dreamed of a Golden Egg.

LITTLE CHICK'S EASTER TREASURE

Easter morning arrived, and Little Chick was up early. She was so excited about the Egg Hunt, the Golden Egg, the Blue Ribbon—OH, EVERYTHING! Her little body shook so!

"Mama! Mama!" she cried. "Oh, please come and help me dress! It's Easter!"

"For heaven's sake, little one, calm down!" Mama Hen said with a laugh. "Why, if you keep shaking so, you're bound to shake yourself right out of your feathers! Now come close; I have a present for you." And Mama Hen showed Little Chick a new Easter dress and straw hat for her to wear.

"OH, THANK YOU, MAMA!" Little Chick chirped with delight. Then Mama Hen helped Little Chick dress for the fair as Papa Redcomb looked on with pride.

The time had come to leave for the Egg Hunt.

LITTLE CHICK'S EASTER TREASURE

Little Chick and her family arrived at the Easter Fair, where all the animals had gathered with their families. EVERYONE was dressed in their Sunday best. And everyone was ready for the Egg Hunt to begin.

LITTLE CHICK'S EASTER TREASURE

Before the Egg Hunt all the young animals gathered close together. The other animals were much older and bigger than Little Chick. They were all talking, each one saying how they would be the one to find the Golden Egg. Jumping up on a tree stump, where everyone could see her, Little Chick chirped out proudly:

"I'm going to be the ONE to find the Golden Egg!"

All the animals burst out laughing, saying: "YOU! FIND THE GOLDEN EGG! Don't be silly. You're far too small!" But Little Chick just folded her little wings and said nothing—certain that she would find the egg and win first prize.

The Great Easter Egg Hunt began. The animals ran in search of the Easter eggs that lay hidden. Eggs were everywhere. They collected blue eggs and green eggs, red eggs and yellow eggs, and just about every color egg imaginable. Some eggs were well hidden in logs and bushes, and some were even up trees. But WHERE was the Golden Egg?

LITTLE CHICK'S EASTER TREASURE

All of the animals ran and collected as many eggs as they could find—all, that is, except Little Chick. She just walked right past the brightly colored eggs. For Little Chick wanted just one egg and one egg only—THE GOLDEN EGG.

LITTLE CHICK'S EASTER TREASURE

Soon Little Chick found herself by a small pond. Had she
wandered too far? Surely the Golden Egg would not be here. But
as she turned to go back up the hill Little Chick heard
something. She stood still and listened, and then she heard a
very loud "BLURP!" She hadn't seen him before, hidden among
the water grasses. Right in front of her was a VERY large and
VERY green bullfrog, resting himself by the edge of the pond.

LITTLE CHICK'S EASTER TREASURE

Little Chick and the Bullfrog stared at each other for what seemed like the LONGEST time. The Bullfrog's large round eyes made her a little nervous.

"Why have you come here, little one?" the Bullfrog croaked. "Don't be afraid. I won't hurt you."

"I . . . I am looking for the Golden Egg," Little Chick replied, still just a bit afraid of the big frog.

"A golden egg? . . . a golden egg," the Bullfrog repeated to himself. "Can you tell me what it looks like?"

"Oh, yes!" Little Chick said excitedly, quite forgetting her fear of the great frog. "Though I have never seen the egg myself, my Grandpa Redcomb told me all about it." And then Little Chick told the Bullfrog all about the Egg Hunt and the Golden Egg. Little Chick chirped with excitement, stretching her little wings out to show the Bullfrog what a big egg it must surely be.

"Why, I KNOW this Golden Egg!" the Bullfrog croaked. "I KNOW it quite well."

LITTLE CHICK'S EASTER TREASURE

"Do you see, little one?" the Bullfrog said as he raised his belly up. AND THERE IT WAS! The Golden Egg. Why, the Bullfrog had been lying on top of it all the time! Little Chick flapped her little wings with joy. Then she stopped.

"But why, Bullfrog?" Little Chick asked, quite puzzled. "Why are you lying on an egg?"

"Well," the Bullfrog began, "I was resting here yesterday just as I am doing now, and down rolled this egg. I stared at it a while, waiting for it to say something. But it never spoke a word. So I got to thinking how smooth it looked. And then I got to thinking how round it looked. And it felt so cool. Now frogs have soft bellies and soft bellies like things that are smooth and round and cool. So I've been resting on it ever since."

"Do you think I could HAVE the Egg?" Little Chick asked.

The Bullfrog rolled his eyes in thought, and then said, "I don't see why not, I always have plenty of cool stones to lie on."

Little Chick CHIRPED with joy.

LITTLE CHICK'S EASTER TREASURE

But there was just one problem. The egg was huge. Almost as big as Little Chick. What COULD she possibly do?

"If I can't carry the Golden Egg," Little Chick thought, "then I will just have to roll it up the hill!"

So Little Chick rolled the Golden Egg slowly up and up and up and UP the hill, till at last she reached the top.

LITTLE CHICK'S EASTER TREASURE

Little Chick rolled the Golden Egg all the way back to the Easter Fair. EVERYONE was so surprised to see that the smallest animal of all had found the biggest egg of all! They gathered round, young and old, and cheered: "HURRAY! Hurray for Little Chick! She has FOUND the Golden Egg!"

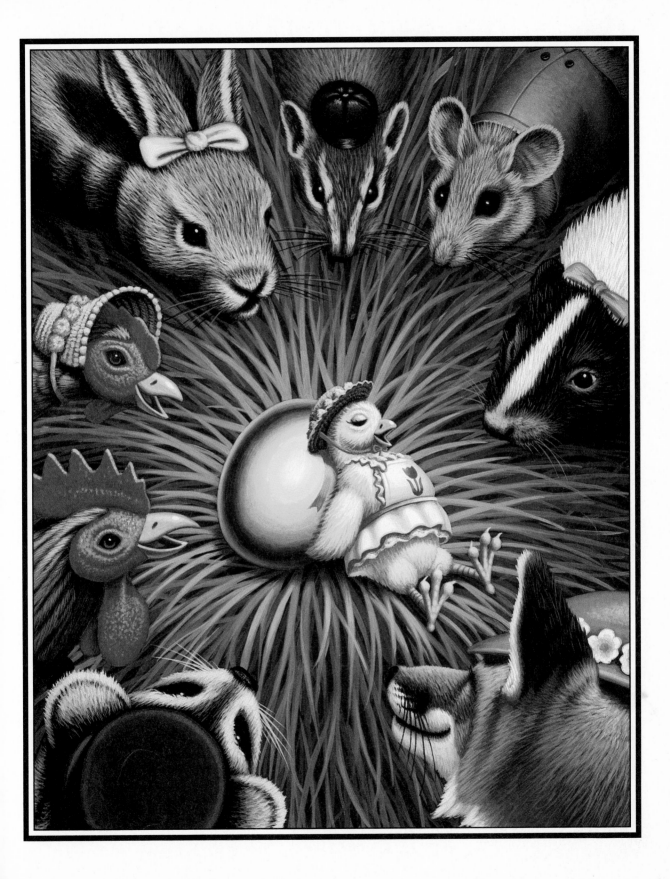

LITTLE CHICK'S EASTER TREASURE

They picked up Little Chick and carried her to the Judge's Table, where she was given the Blue Ribbon as FIRST prize. Everyone cheered as the Judge pinned the ribbon on Little Chick's dress. But JUST as the Judge was about to speak—the Golden Egg moved! All by itself! Everyone waited to see what would happen next. The Golden Egg moved again . . . and again . . . and again . . . and then . . .

THE EGG HATCHED!

LITTLE CHICK'S EASTER TREASURE

A GOLDEN CHICK. A beautiful Golden Chick had hatched from the Golden Egg! The animals cheered—Little Chick most of all. For Little Chick knew something wonderful had happened. Why, not only had she won the Blue Ribbon, but she had also FOUND a friend.

LITTLE CHICK'S EASTER TREASURE

The BUSY day finally came to an end. Little Chick told her new friend all about the Great Easter Egg Hunt—and said perhaps next year—yes, next year, Golden Chick would be the ONE to find the Golden Egg. Wing in wing, the two new friends set out for home.

For over a decade, Unicorn has been publishing
richly illustrated editions of classic and contemporary
works for children and adults. To continue this tradition,
WE WOULD LIKE TO KNOW WHAT YOU THINK.

If you would like to send us your suggestions or obtain
a list of our current titles, please write to:
THE UNICORN PUBLISHING HOUSE, INC.
P.O. Box 377
Morris Plains, NJ   07950
ATT: Dept CLP

Printing History 15 14 13 12 11 10 9 8 7 6 5 4 3 2

Library of Congress Cataloging-in-Publication Data

Shaw, Samantha, 1959-
    Little Chick's Easter Treasure / illustrated by Walt Sturrock; story by Samantha Shaw.
        p. cm. — (Through the magic window)
    Summary: A little chick celebrates her first Easter by going on an egg hunt and finding a
very special egg.

    [1. Easter eggs—Fiction. 2. Chickens—Fiction.] I. Sturrock, Walt, 1961-   ill. II. Title.
III. Series.
PZ7.S53434Li   1991
[E]—dc20
                                                                          90-11303
                                                                          CIP
                                                                          AC

This book is dedicated to
my grandmother, Emily Sturrock,
for her endless love of all children.